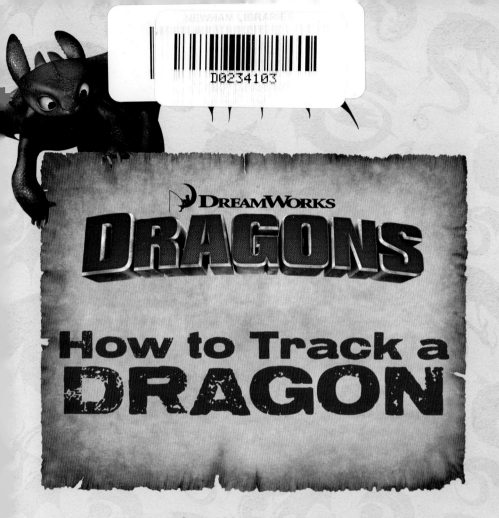

DreamWorks DRAGONS

How to Track a DRAGON

adapted by Erica David

Hodder
Children's
Books

HODDER CHILDREN'S BOOKS

First published by Simon Spotlight
An imprint of Simon & Schuster Children's Publishing Division
1230 Avenue of the Americas, New York, New York 10020

First published in Great Britain in 2017 by Hodder and Stoughton

A CIP catalogue record for this book
is available from the British Library.

ISBN 978 1 444 93434 2

Printed and bound in China by RR Donnelley Asia Printing Solutions Limited

The paper and board used in this book are made from wood from responsible sources

MIX
Paper from
responsible sources
FSC® C104740

Hodder Children's Books
An imprint of
Hachette Children's Group
Part of Hodder and Stoughton
Carmelite House
50 Victoria Embankment
London EC4Y 0DZ

An Hachette UK Company
www.hachette.co.uk

www.hachettechildrens.co.uk

There was trouble at Dragon's Edge.
A Rumblehorn dragon was up to no good.
Every night it attacked the Dragon
Riders' fort.

Hiccup and his friends set a trap.
They wanted to catch the dragon.
Instead, they caught Gobber!

Gobber had come from Berk to talk to
Hiccup.

He explained that Hiccup's father,
Stoick, was shouting at everyone.
"He's driving the village crazy!"

Hiccup had to go back to Berk. He had to find out what was wrong with Stoick.

He didn't want to leave with a Rumblehorn on the loose, but his dad was more important.

When Hiccup got to Berk, he heard his
dad shouting.

"I said I wanted these weapons arranged
by deadliness!" Stoick yelled as he
stomped away.

Hiccup followed his dad across the village. Stoick was being very hard on everyone.

He even yelled at a nice old woman named Gothi. "You plow like an old woman!" he shouted at her.

Hiccup soon realised what was wrong. Stoick wouldn't admit it, but he missed his old dragon, Thornado. He spent a lot of time keeping Thornado's saddle nice and shiny.

Hiccup had an idea. He asked his dad to help with the Rumblehorn dragon. Stoick loved a challenge! It would make him feel better.

Meanwhile, back at Dragon's Edge, Gobber hatched a plan. He and the Dragon Riders built a giant wall to keep the Rumblehorn away.

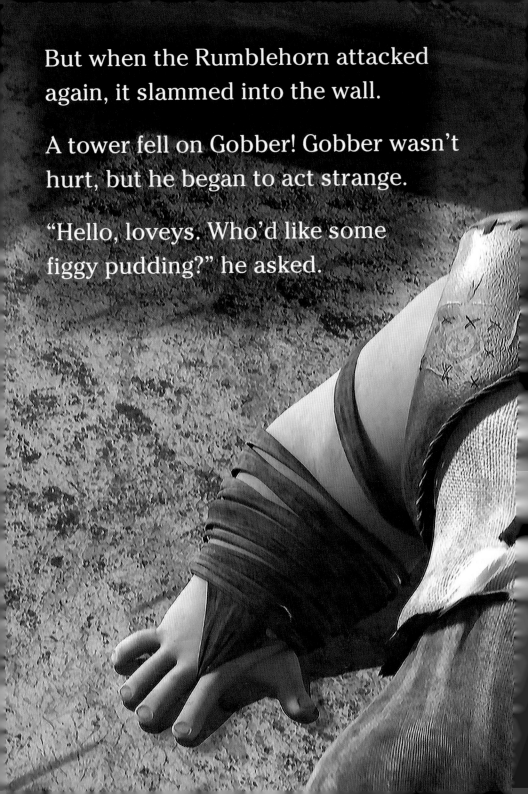

But when the Rumblehorn attacked
again, it slammed into the wall.

A tower fell on Gobber! Gobber wasn't
hurt, but he began to act strange.

"Hello, loveys. Who'd like some
figgy pudding?" he asked.

"Hiccup, these Rumblehorn attacks are getting out of hand," Astrid said when Hiccup and Stoick arrived.

Hiccup took charge. He sent everyone out to search for the Rumblehorn.

Hiccup and Stoick tracked the dragon through the forest.

"These footprints are fresh," said Hiccup. "We should be right on top of the Rumblehorn."

"It's like the beast can sense us coming, and then it changes direction," said Stoick.

Stoick had an idea for how to draw the dragon out. He sang loudly and beat the ground.

Soon the Rumblehorn appeared. Stoick charged and lassoed the dragon with his rope.

But the Rumblehorn didn't give up.
It took off into the air with Stoick
hanging onto the rope!

The Rumblehorn flew higher and higher.
Stoick tried to hold on, but his hands
slipped and he fell through the air!

Hiccup and Toothless flew to the rescue!

They caught Stoick, and then they raced back to the fort. What they didn't know was that now the Rumblehorn was following them!

At the fort Gobber was still acting strange. He had even painted his face!

Suddenly the Rumblehorn swooped in and it started following Gobber! Gobber was still out of it. He didn't see that he was in danger.

Hiccup and the others tried to protect Gobber. Astrid's dragon, Stormfly, fired spikes at the Rumblehorn. But the Rumblehorn wouldn't stop.

Everyone was worried. They thought the Rumblehorn would hurt Gobber.

But suddenly it stopped and roared in Gobber's face.

"I think this dragon is trying to tell us something," Stoick said.

Slowly, he walked toward the Rumblehorn. "What is it you really want, dragon?" asked Stoick.

The Rumblehorn roared again. It tossed
Stoick onto its back and zoomed off into
the sky. The other dragons took flight.

From up high, Hiccup saw the problem.
A giant wave was headed for the island!
The Rumblehorn had been trying
to warn them!

Hiccup, Stoick, and the Dragon Riders sped into action. They built up Gobber's rock wall. They made it longer and stronger to block the wave.

The giant wave crashed into the wall and the wall cracked!

The dragons and their riders worked hard to plug the cracks and the Rumblehorn helped too! The fort was safe!

Later everyone was thankful for the Rumblehorn.

"If he hadn't been so hardheaded, we would've been wiped out," Hiccup said.

Stoick smiled at the Rumblehorn. "He is hardheaded, just like me," he said.

Stoick petted his new dragon. "I think I'll call you Skullcrusher," he told him.

Skullcrusher snorted happily. He and Stoick made a great team.